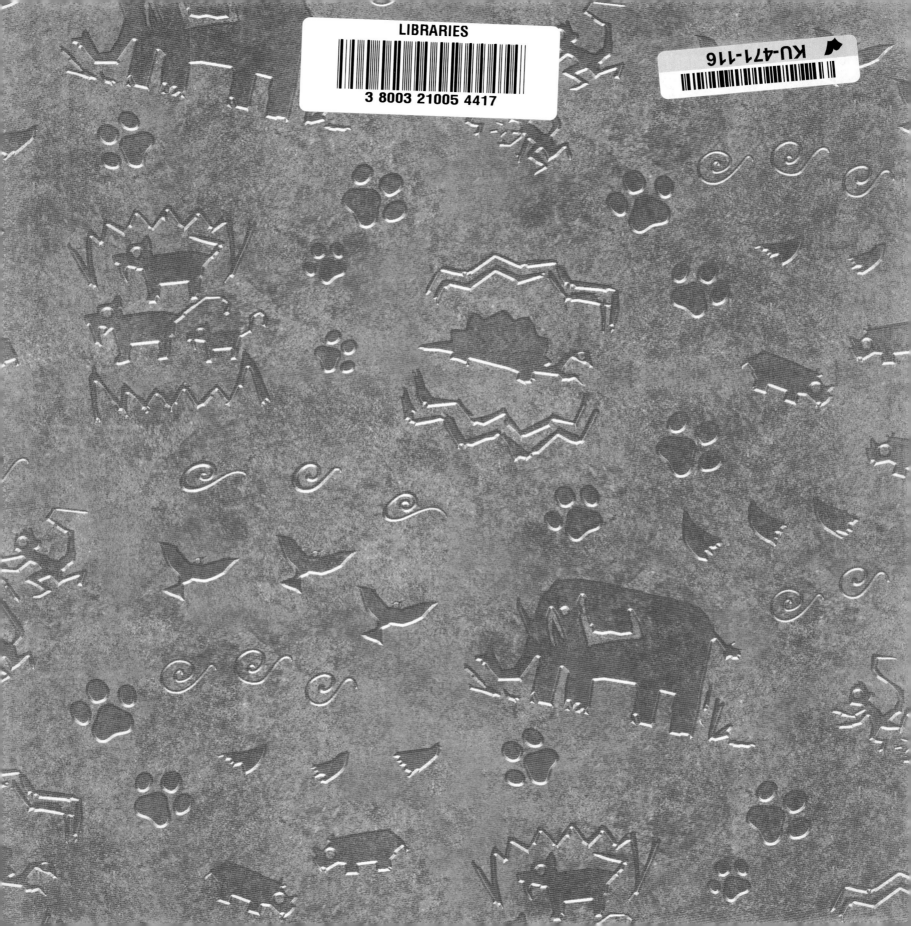

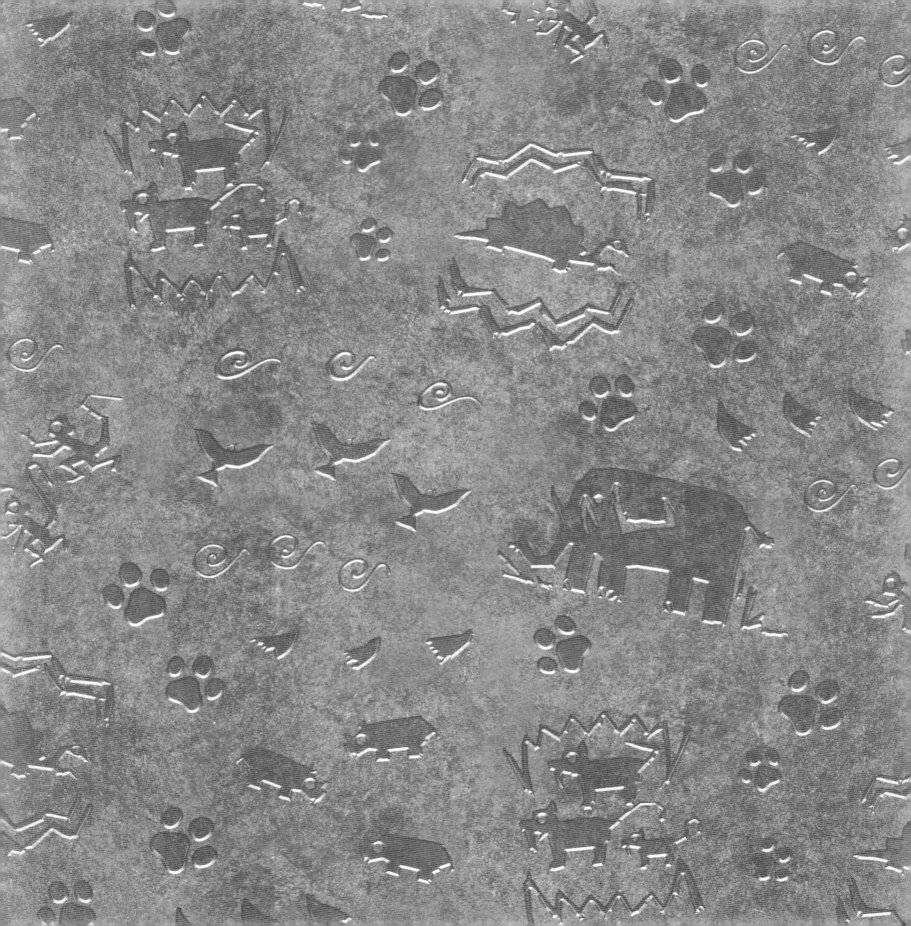

This storybook belongs to

....

First published in the United States by Penguin Random House 2024
This edition published in Great Britain 2024 by Farshore
An imprint of HarperCollins*Publishers*
1 London Bridge Street, London SE1 9GF
www.farshore.co.uk

HarperCollins*Publishers*
Macken House, 39/40 Mayor Street Upper,
Dublin 1, D01 C9W8, Ireland

Written by Frank Berrios
Based on the teleplay 'Jungle Pups Save the Big, Big Animals' by Louise Moon
Illustrated by Nate Lovett
Additional cover illustrations by MJ Illustrations

ISBN 978 0 00 861532 1
Printed in the United Kingdom
001

A CIP catalogue record for this title is available from the British Library.

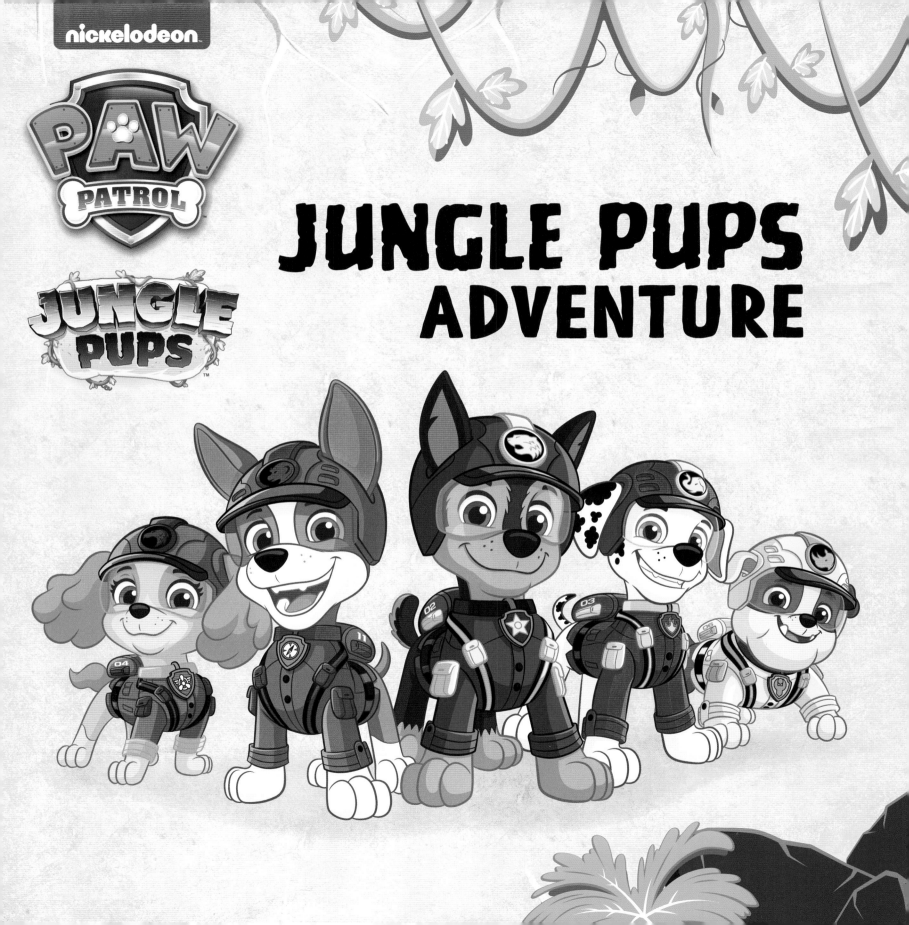

JUNGLE PUPS ADVENTURE

Early one morning, Ryder and the PAW Patrol pups were busy gathering treats for their jungle friends.

"The Hidden Jungle is such a magical place!" said Ryder.

"I can't wait to learn more about it!" replied Carlos. "I'm heading to the cave to study the old drawings in there."

Meanwhile, Marshall went to look for their animal
friends, but they were hiding in the bushes.
"There you are!" said Marshall, spotting some worried-looking elephants.
"Are you hiding from something?"

Suddenly, Marshall tripped and fell into what he thought was a huge hole.
Then he realised it wasn't a hole at all . . .
"Whoa! This is a really big paw print," he said. "No wonder the elephants
are afraid!"

Marshall told Ryder about the scared animals and the big paw print.

"Don't worry," said Ryder. "We'll find out what's frightening them. No paw print is too big, no pup is too small!" he added. "Jungle Pups to the PAW Patroller!" Ryder gave the pups their assignments.

"Skye!" he said. "Fly over the jungle to see if you can find whatever made that paw print. Marshall! Talk to the animals and find out why they're so scared. Chase! Use your detective skills to investigate the print. Jungle pups are on a roll!"

Ryder and Chase went to see the paw print.
"ACHOO!" sneezed Chase. "Some kind of cat must have made this.
It looks like a tiger print, but I've never seen one this big."

Marshall went to check on the elephants, but spotted a huge animal nearby.
"Nice gigantic kitty-cat!" he said. "I'm Marshall. What's your name?"
The animal snarled . . . and then roared loudly! Marshall and his elephant
friend ran away.

"Strange," Marshall panted, when he was sure the animal was gone.

"That big tiger was limping. I wonder if it's hurt."

Just then, Ryder and Chase arrived. "Marshall? We heard a growl.

Are you okay?"

Marshall told them about the huge cat with long, curved fangs.

"That sounds like a sabre-toothed tiger!" said Ryder.

Ryder called Carlos, who told him that big cats had lived in the area a long time ago.

"How could an ancient cat be running around the jungle now?" asked Ryder.

"I don't know," replied Carlos. "The Hidden Jungle is full of mysteries."

"This is one mystery we need to solve," said Chase.
"Ryder to Jungle Pups. Be on the lookout for a sabre-toothed tiger.
We need to keep it away from the other animals and find out how
it got here."

Marshall and his elephant friend headed further into the jungle, and soon spotted a cloud that was hovering close to the ground. "That's an odd-looking cloud," said Marshall. Suddenly, he and the elephant slipped down an icy cliff!

"What happened to all the trees? **BRRR!** It's chilly down here!"
said Marshall, after they had safely landed in a valley.
Skye soon spotted them from the sky.

"I see a valley!" Skye reported to Ryder. "It doesn't look like the rest of the jungle, though. It's all frozen!"

Marshall explored the valley. Storm clouds had started circling in the sky, but a few rays of sunlight peeked through and landed on some ice chunks. Suddenly, the ice melted, revealing real, live woolly mammoths! "Uh-oh, those shaggy ice elephants look thirsty and hungry," said Marshall. "Run!"

He and the elephant started to run.

"Ryder, I think I found the place where the sabre-toothed tiger came from – along with some other animals that have just thawed out!" Marshall yelled into his Pup Tag.

"Maybe a long time ago, the whole Hidden Jungle was hit by a sudden ice storm!" said Ryder, arriving at the edge of the cliff. "Then most of the jungle warmed up later, but this valley has stayed frozen until now."

"The sabre-toothed tiger must have thawed first," said Chase.

"Now the others are thawing, too."

Tracker used the cables on his monkey jeep to lower himself down into the valley. Suddenly, a huge ape appeared! Tracker and his monkey friends tossed it bananas.

"I never met a monkey who didn't like bananas!" chuckled Tracker.

The pups needed to find a way to thaw the valley and save the animals'
home. Then Marshall spotted the limping sabre-toothed tiger again.
"Do you have a sore paw, kitty? Maybe I can help," he said.
Ryder called the pups on his Pup Pad. "PAW Patrol, can I get an update?"

"We need to hurry, the storm clouds are getting darker!" said Marshall.

"And bigger!" added Skye. "They could cover the entire Hidden Jungle."

"We need to find enough heat to warm up the valley and stop the storm," replied Ryder. Then he had an idea!

"The volcano!" he said. "We need to send some
hot volcano gases over to the frozen valley to melt all the ice."
Rubble, Tracker and Rocky dug an underground tunnel. The plan worked!
The ice thawed and the storm clouds cleared up.

"Now that the valley is unfrozen, I'm sure the big, ancient animals will be happy to stay down here," said Ryder.

Marshall even made a new friend – when he pulled a thorn out of the big tiger's paw!

HOORAY FOR THE JUNGLE PUPS!

Collect these other pup-tacular PAW Patrol stories!